TOUCHED
BY AN
ANGEL

Doodlebugs

"Do you think your dad and Ada will *ever* get together, Jess?" asked Bits.

"Yes!" said Jessie. "They have to. They just *have* to!"

TOUCHED
BY AN
ANGEL

Doodlebugs

Novelization by Monica Hall
Based on a teleplay by
Ken LaZebnik

Martha Williamson
Executive Producer

Based on the television
series created by
John Masius

Thomas Nelson, Inc.
Nashville

Doodlebugs
Book Four in the *Touched By An Angel* fiction series.

Touched By An Angel is a trademark of CBS Broadcasting Inc. Used under license.

This novelization of *Doodlebugs* by Monica Hall is based on a teleplay of the same title by Ken LaZebnik.

Published in Nashville, Tennessee, by Tommy Nelson™, a division of Thomas Nelson, Inc. Vice President, Children's Books: Laura Minchew; Managing Editor: Beverly Phillips.

Library of Congress Cataloging-in-Publication Data

Hall, Monica.
    Doodlebugs / novelization by Monica Hall ; based on a teleplay by Ken LaZebnik ; Martha Williamson, executive producer.
       p. cm.—(Touched by an angel)
    "Based on the television series created by John Masius."
    Summary: While Jessie schemes to get her widower dad married, a mysterious voice on the local pay phone has people thinking God is advising them. But angels from God and a lesson about doodlebugs reveal the truth.
    ISBN 0-8499-5805-9
    [1. Guardian angels—Fiction. 2. Angels—Fiction. 3. Christian life—Fiction.] I. LaZebnik, Ken. II. Touched by an angel (Television program) III. Title. IV. Series.
PZ7.H14725Do 1999
[Fic]—dc21

                        99–10328
                           CIP

Printed in the United States of America

99 00 01 02 03 QPV 9 8 7 6 5 4 3 2 1

Contents

Contents

The Characters

Jessie Hughes, a bright, resourceful twelve-year-old with more than a little imagination. Her plan to find a wife for her father sets the town on its ear.

Bits Brydon, a curious ten-year-old whirlwind who is Jessie's best friend. Nothing escapes Bits's notice—especially when it comes to Jessie and her matchmaking schemes.

Pearhead, a somewhat slow man in his twenties, who always has a solution—usually the wrong one—for everything.

Ada Dobbins, a warm, loving woman with a beautiful voice, and a heart to match.

Erskine Hughes, Jessie's father and the town's former minister. A gentle, troubled man who is searching for meaning in his life.

Sis Winslow, a brisk, no-nonsense woman who wants to do something big in life, but doesn't think she'll ever get the chance.

Vinegar Winslow, Sis's brother. He is a shy man whose quietness conceals a courage that surprises everyone.

The Characters

Tess, a take-charge, problem-solving angel, who is unexpectedly "bugged" by one very big challenge and a lot of pesky little ones.

Monica, a joyful angel who embraces life with wonder and delight.

Andrew, an angel of many talents, including—as it turns out—telephone repair.

Introduction

Jessie's fingers flew over the keys, then she pressed 'enter' and stood up. The computer hummed—busy with its research—while Jessie wandered aimlessly around her room.

She pushed a dangling cable back into a tangle of electronic gear, poked at a disassembled radio, and adjusted the big brass telescope at the window. But nothing held her interest. Jessie couldn't seem to settle down to any one thing tonight. Even this year's science fair project about NASA—her most spectacular ever—didn't look too interesting.

As two unseen visitors watched from the window seat, Jessie turned to the mirror with a sigh. Dark eyes frowning, she studied her reflection. Then she made a face, and stuck out her tongue. Thirteen next week, and she was still all elbows, knees, and braces!

Oh, Mama, she thought, *even you would be disappointed in how your swan is turning out.* 'Swan' . . . that's what her beautiful mother had always called her. "Be patient, my swan," she'd say. "You're going to wake up one morning, and you won't believe your eyes!"

Well, it had better happen soon. I don't have much time left!

BEEP! The computer screen flickered, then filled with data.

Monica peered over Jessie's shoulder. "Oh, Tess, does she have—"

"Cancer?" Tess finished. "Well, *she* thinks she does, and nobody can convince her otherwise. That young lady has quite an imagination!" Tess's voice grew gentle. "Jessie's mother died of cancer two years ago, and Jessie's positive she has it, too. She misses her mother, and worries about her father being all alone when she's gone. And what bothers her most is that she doesn't know what to do about it."

"Is our assignment to help Jessie?" Monica asked.

Tess sighed. "Angel Girl, this whole town is our assignment. Trouble is, I'm just not sure yet what God wants us to do!"

Chapter One

Creatures
Great and Small

The Georgia wind ran curious fingers through the treetops, then wandered lazily down Main Street. Stirring a piece of paper here; swirling up a dust devil there; tugging at the shuttered windows of the empty little church. Then, with a farewell rattle at the door of the old phone booth, it left the little town alone to doze in the sun.

Now, nothing moved in the midday heat, not even Bits Brydon—and that was very unusual. The curious ten-year-old with the flyaway copper curls rarely lit anywhere for more than a moment. In fact, Bits was the closest thing that Hope, Georgia, had to a perpetual-motion machine!

But right now she knelt, still as a stone, beside a tiny hole in the ground. Eyes intent, she held a long pine needle just above the opening. Barely moving her fingers, Bits gave it just the tiniest little twitch.

"Hey, Bits. How ya doing?" boomed a voice behind her.

Bits jumped, jerked around, and fell over. She glared at the young man grinning down at

2

her, then reluctantly smiled. "Hey, Pearhead."

Sometimes people made fun of Pearhead because he was a little slow to understand things. But not Bits. Goodness knows, 'cept for Pearhead and her best friend, Jessie, there weren't all that many people left to talk with in this town!

"Whatcha doing?" he asked.

"Catchin' doodlebugs," she answered. "Least I'm trying to. Not having much luck."

"Oh, that's easy," he assured her. Pearhead always had a solution, but the trouble was his solutions hardly ever worked out the way he expected. "You stick a cheese square on your pine needle," he told her. "Some of that Monterey Jack. They love that."

Bits nodded as Pearhead strolled on down Main Street. *Monterey Jack cheese? Wait till Jessie hears this!* And Bits was off in a flash to look for her friend.

Monica looked out from her seat in the old gazebo to the shuttered church across the square. "Oh, Tess, there's nothing sadder than a church that's been deserted."

"You got that right, baby," Tess answered. "Nothing left in there but the bugs." She glanced down at the bench they shared. "And speaking of bugs," she said, sliding away, "there's a caterpillar on this book!"

Careful not to disturb its tiny passenger, Monica picked up the book. "Look how slowly that wee fella's movin', Tess. I think I'll call him Moses."

Tess widened the space between them a little more. "Never mind that caterpillar, you've got a lot of watching and reading to do, Angel Girl."

"Watching? Reading? But what about my assignment?" asked Monica.

"That *is* your assignment," said Tess. "Just sit here and keep an eye on this town. Something's going on here and we've got to figure it out."

"What about the reading part?" Monica asked.

"Well," said Tess, "maybe the clue to this mystery is in that book."

"Mystery?" echoed Monica, looking at the book's title. "Plato?" Then her eyes lit up. "Oh, I remember that Greek philosopher. Such a wise man, Tess." She frowned. "He talked about the difference between what *is* real and what we only *think is* real."

Tess nodded. "We've both got a puzzle to solve this time, baby. Yours is in that book and watching. Mine . . ." she said, nose wrinkling, "is out in the field with the bugs!"

Monica had never seen Tess look so uncomfortable. "What *is* your assignment?"

Tess sighed. "That's the puzzle. God has given me a real challenge. This whole town's falling apart. First the church closed. Then everybody lost sight of the light. Now they've become afraid of taking responsibility for themselves. So they're all hunkered down like doodlebugs, waiting for God to pluck 'em up and out! And the only clue I have to the puzzle is bugs! And, Angel Girl," Tess finished, her eyes snapping wide open, "I don't like bugs!"

"Tess!" Monica was shocked.

Tess looked a little embarrassed. "I know,

bugs are God's creatures, too. I'm working on my attitude. But meanwhile, the bugs and I have an arrangement: I don't mess with them, and they don't mess with me!"

It would take a pretty brave bug to mess with Tess, thought Monica. She choked back a giggle as Tess stalked out of the gazebo. "Oh, look at her, Moses," she whispered to the caterpillar, "waving that net around, wearing that vest with all those pockets. All she needs now is a safari helmet."

Monica gently stroked the caterpillar. "She didn't really mean that about not liking bugs," she assured him. "She just hasn't had a chance to get to know any of you."

Moses arched his back against her stroking finger, but he didn't look very convinced.

Chapter Two

Astonishments

Pearhead strolled slowly down Main Street, then stopped to watch a butterfly investigate a patch of wildflowers. *I wonder what I'll do today?* he thought.

RING!

Pearhead jumped. A telephone on Main Street?

RING! RING! RING!

It sure was—in that old phone booth on the corner!

"Didn't even know that thing could ring," he muttered, hurrying over. He picked up the receiver. "Hello?"

"Pearhead," said a very strange voice, all boomy and whispery at the same time.

Pearhead's mouth dropped open. "You . . . you got him."

The voice rolled on like distant thunder. "You live in a trailer. You sell ice cream out of a broken van. You don't know where your next dime's coming from."

Pearhead jerked the phone from his ear and yelled in the receiver, "Who is this?"

But the voice wasn't finished. "Here's what you do. Go to Sis and Vinegar's restaurant. Look under the watering can by the bench out front. You'll find a scratched-off lottery ticket worth fifty dollars. It's the start of your nest egg."

Pearhead almost forgot to breathe. "Fifty dollars! Who is this?"

"That is not for you to know. I'll call back." And the line went dead.

Pearhead stared at the phone, then he looked up and down the empty street. *Somebody's playin' another joke on me. Well, this time I'm not going to fall for it! No sir!* He hung up with a bang, peeled a stick of gum, and again strolled off down Main Street—whistling. *That'll show 'em!*

But it sure was hard to act casual as he passed Sis and Vinegar's restaurant. That old bench out in front was real hard to ignore. And there *was* a rusty old watering can sitting there.

Do you suppose . . . ? Could it be . . . ? He wondered.

The spicy aroma of barbecue teased the noses of the morning regulars at Sis and Vinegar's restaurant. Sooner or later, just about everybody in town dropped by for the coffee and the company, or to comment on the latest checkers game between old Mr. Porter and Grandpa Willis.

Behind the counter, Sis Winslow smiled as Grandpa Willis hooted and kinged another checker. Then she brushed a gleaming black curl from her forehead with slender brown fingers, and looked over at her brother's table and sighed.

Ignoring everything around him, Vinegar was hard at work on his newest birdhouse. *Lost in his own little world again,* thought Sis sadly as Vinegar dipped a careful brush into bright blue paint. *I need to decide soon what Vinegar and I will do! Well, I'm not the only one with problems,* she reminded herself with a glance at one of her favorite customers.

Ada Dobbins sure doesn't seem her usual sunny, talkative self today! Sis studied the small blonde woman with the sweet face and golden voice.

Ada smiled wistfully as she looked around the cozy little cafe. She'd miss this place. But her plans were made! She turned the page of the Atlanta newspaper. *Now, if I can just find an apartment I can afford . . .*

Sque-e-e-a-k . . . BANG! The screen door flew open and slammed into the wall. Everyone jumped. Ada's coffee splattered onto her paper. Three checkers bounced to the floor. And Vinegar's brush skittered a jagged blue line up the birdhouse.

"Hey, everybody," crowed Pearhead, "I won the lottery!"

"Well, good for you!" cheered Ada.

"All good things come to him that waits," said Pearhead, waving the lottery ticket. "And I've been waiting for this a long time."

Ada's blue eyes danced. "I believe your ship's come in, Pearhead. You planning to retire in style now?" she teased.

"Maybe!" Pearhead answered back.

"Let me see that," said Sis, plucking the ticket from Pearhead's fingers. Sis stared at the amount on the ticket, then raised an eyebrow. "Fifty dollars? You're going to retire on fifty dollars?"

But Pearhead was as excited as ever. "It's the start of my nest egg, Sis. I'm fixing up my ice-cream van, then you just watch!" He bounced across the room. "Vinegar, look here. I'm a winner."

Vinegar dabbed at the smeared paint. "So this town's got a winner, huh? You could've fooled me. You bought a good ticket."

Pearhead shook his head. "No, I found it! This voice tipped me off."

Sis rolled her eyes at Ada. "This week he's hearing voices!"

"Well, I don't see you winning anything, Sis," Pearhead answered. "You're just digging a hole of debt around here."

"Six feet deep and getting deeper," Sis agreed, with a glance toward Vinegar. "And since I'm the only one doing any work around here . . ."

Vinegar answered softly. "I'm working on my birdhouses, Sis."

Sis sighed. She'd hurt his feelings, again. She turned, relieved as the back door creaked open and Tess stepped in. "Oh, there you are," Sis said, eyeing Tess doubtfully. She looked like someone who knew what she was doing. *Still . . . a butterfly net?* "You really think you can get rid of these ants?"

Tess knew she could. "No problem," she answered, studying the line of ants marching across the kitchen floor. Then she opened the screen door. "Okay," she said sternly, "go on. Move out. Get your little ant behinds out of here!"

Sis's mouth dropped open. *She's going to talk those ants out?!* Then her chin dropped even farther, because the ant parade was making a perfect about-face and heading for the back door!

"Out the door, and around the corner," directed Tess. "I've got a hole for you. Go on now. Go!"

No one breathed as they watched the obedient little line march across the threshold.

"Wow," said Vinegar.

"That's amazing!" agreed Sis.

"See?" said Pearhead. "Anything can happen. Ants can turn around and leave. This strange voice on the pay phone clues me in to winning fifty dollars. It's like a miracle."

But Sis wasn't convinced. "So, I suppose you think that pay phone is a pipeline to heaven, huh?"

"Really?" said Tess, both eyebrows raised.

But Pearhead didn't get a chance to respond.

"What's going on?" called a voice at the front door. "Whoops! Careful, Jessie," Erskine Hughes said as he caught the big potted fern his daughter had bumped into.

Sis smiled at the newcomers. "Hello, Jessie. Erskine. This is a nice surprise. Haven't seen much of you lately."

The tall man with the gentle face smiled back. "Well, you know how it is, been busy."

Ever since Erskine's wife had died and he had left the ministry, Erskine had kept more and more to himself. Sis suspected that coming in today was Jessie's idea. And Sis thought she knew why.

The little redhead peeping through the front window knew why, too. In fact, there wasn't much that went on in town that Bits didn't know. It wasn't that she was *nosy*, mind you, just *interested*.

Like Sis, Bits especially enjoyed watching all the ways Jessie found to get her father and Ada together. Jessie thought that Ada would be a perfect wife for her dad and a wonderful mom, too. Ada was beautiful all the way through—the way she looked, the way she sang, and the way she always had time to listen to Jessie!

I wonder what Jessie's plan is now, thought Bits, grinning. *It'll be hard to beat that 'floating picnic'—even though that old raft did come apart! Or the time Jessie decided the town needed a recycling program—with Ada's potting shed as the drop-off point and Jessie's father doing the hauling. Jessie had figured with all her dad's trips back and forth that he would be seeing Ada a lot. It would have worked, too, if on the first haul he hadn't accidentally recycled Ada's prized collection of antique flowerpots! Such a shame,* Bits thought. *Ada is usually a good sport about these things.*

Chapter Three

Believers and Skeptics

Jessie was still shaking her head over the ant story as she slid into a chair at Ada's table. "'Lo, Ada," she said beaming, motioning for her father to join them.

Ada smiled back. "Good morning, Jessie. How are you?"

"Well," said Jessie seriously, "pretty good today. But I may be in the hospital by next week. You never know."

Oh dear! What do I say to that? Ada wondered, looking at Erskine, who just rolled his eyes.

Jessie sighed. *They don't believe I have cancer either. Well, just because the doctors and my dad say nothing's wrong that doesn't change anything. A person knows when a person has something!*

"Hey, Jessie," called Vinegar, "the microwave broke. Can you take a look?"

A microwave? She'd been wanting to work on one of those! Jessie loved to tinker. And there wasn't much—mechanical or electronic— that she hadn't taught herself how to fix.

"Sure, Vinegar, be glad to check it out," she answered, already on her way to the kitchen.

"Can I watch?" asked Bits, appearing out of thin air as she often seemed to do.

"Sure," came the answer.

"Unplug it first, Jessie," her father called after them.

"Well, of course, Dad!"

"I guess she's feeling a mite better," Ada said with a laugh.

Erskine grinned back. "You know Jessie: give her something to fix or a computer to work on and she's right as rain. How are you doing, Ada?"

She gave him her most cheerful smile, and tapped her newspaper. "Looking for a place in Atlanta. I've got a waitress job lined up at a fancy restaurant. And they might have room for another singer, too."

Ada's leaving? Erskine didn't know what to say. Jessie would really miss her. And so would . . . well, they'd all miss her. But he knew how much her singing meant to her.

"Well, I hope they do, Ada." he said. "They'd be crazy not to."

Disappointed, Ada looked down at her paper. She really thought a lot of Erskine and had hoped he'd ask her to stay. "So, Erskine," she asked, "are you getting along okay?"

He shrugged. "You know—just taking things one day at a time."

"Maybe another church will need a wonderful pastor," Ada offered.

"There's nothing wrong with driving a truck," Erskine answered. "Maybe that's all God really wants me to do."

"Oh, Erskine . . ." Ada began.

But Erskine didn't want sympathy, so he changed the subject. "Hey, Vinegar," he called, "that your latest?"

Vinegar held up the ornate little birdhouse. "Yeah. It's for a blue warbler. But you never know who's really going to move in. You never know nothin' in this life."

"That's right," chimed in Pearhead. "Ants marching. Phones ringing. Only God knows what all else."

"Apparently so!" grumbled Tess at her table in the corner. She winced as something crashed and clattered in the kitchen. *Is Jessie fixing that microwave or demolishing it?*

Nobody else paid any attention. They were all used to the sounds of Jessie-at-work.

***

"Whoops!" said Bits, scrambling after the metal mixing bowls spinning across the kitchen floor.

Rubbing her elbow, Jessie bent to pick up some scattered mail. *What a silly place for Sis to stack the mail, right where I need to work! I'll have to build her a letter holder.*

"You ready for this now?" asked Bits.

"Hmm . . . what?" said Jessie, slowly stuffing a letter back into its envelope and restacking the mail on the counter.

"This," said Bits, holding out a screwdriver.

"Uh . . . not yet," said Jessie. "I still have to fix this wiring."

"Jessie, if you live to be an astronaut, will you have to fix a lot of things?"

"I sure hope so, Bits."

Bits watched patiently with admiring eyes until Jessie finally tightened the last screw, plugged in the microwave, and turned it on. "You know, Jess," she teased, "you're almost as good at fixing stuff as you are at breaking it."

Jessie grinned back. "Now, Bits, I didn't exactly break that control on Ada's power mower. I just fixed it so it wouldn't work. There's a difference, you know."

Bits giggled. "And she did call your dad for help, just like you planned. 'Course there was that one little problem . . ."

Jessie shook her head. "I don't know what he did to that thing. It sure wasn't supposed to take off that fast! Ada was really miffed about her flower beds."

"Never mind," consoled Bits. "You'll think of something else. You always do. Hey, want to catch some doodlebugs after lunch?"

"Uh . . . not today, Bits," said Jessie, checking her watch. "I've . . . I've got some stuff to do in my room. Maybe tomorrow." And she was out the door.

Bits looked after her, frowning. She knew that look! Jessie was up to something.

When the lunchtime rush was over, Sis marched Pearhead to the old phone booth. "Okay. We're going to check this out right now!" She dropped in a quarter. "Operator? Could you trace the last call made to this pay phone? . . . Yes, I'll hold."

Tess strolled casually across the street to join Bits, busy looking in a hole in the ground behind the phone booth. "What are you doing, sugar?"

"Tryin' to catch doodlebugs," said Bits.

"That's interesting," said Tess. "I'm an entomologist myself."

"What's that?" asked Bits.

"Someone who studies bugs," answered Tess, as if she thought it was a good idea. "In fact, I'm here studying doodlebugs."

"So you know what they really are?" asked Bits.

"Well . . . sure," answered Tess. "They're bugs."

"They're really antlion larvae," Bits informed her. "They burrow in the sand and wait for ants to fall in. Ants are their breakfast, lunch, and dinner," she explained with relish.

"Of course," said Tess quickly. "I knew that. Did your mama teach you all that?"

"Yes, ma'am," said Bits. "And you know what else? She said when the time is right the doodlebugs are gonna transform—whatever that means."

"Well," said Tess, watching Sis hang up the phone, "I hope to see some transforming around here myself." And with that Tess moved a little closer to the phone booth.

"Well, that was a waste of time," Sis told Pearhead. "They can't trace the call. And I've got work waiting." But she had barely started across the street when . . .

RING!

Pearhead reached it first. "Hello?" He listened a moment, then handed the phone to Sis. "It's for you."

Sis took the phone as if she thought it might bite—and in a way it did.

"My child," said that deep, faraway voice, "when you were growing up in Detroit, you knew that your brother, Vincent, rarely gave the right answer to anything, and so the other kids made fun of him. That turned him sour. That's how he got the nickname Vinegar."

"Who . . . who am I talking to?" Sis sputtered.

But the voice went right on. "No one realized Vincent couldn't hear well until he was grown. Even after the operation fixed his hearing, no one treated him differently. When your grandfather died and left you the restaurant, you brought Vinegar to Georgia hoping for a new start. But the restaurant is losing money, and to make money you need to expand the building and modernize the kitchen. But the bank turned down your request for a loan."

Sis was stunned. *How did the voice know? I just opened the letter from the bank this morning.* "I . . . I don't know what to do," she admitted.

"First things first," came the answer. "You

had a fight with Vinegar last week. What you need to do is go and say you're sorry. Then he'll hug you, the way he always does, and you'll both feel better. Do that, my child, then I'll call back."

Sis stood very still, ignoring Pearhead's anxious questions: "He said something, didn't he? See? See!" insisted Pearhead.

Chapter Four

More Questions Than Answers

Cicadas and peepers tuned up their Georgia night song outside Jessie's window, but she didn't hear a note of it. Every bit of her attention was focused on her computer screen.

Her father knocked softly on her door and then cracked it and leaned into the room. "It's late, Jessie. What are you looking at, anyway?"

"Uh . . . just some research, Dad," she said, quickly hitting the 'escape' key so he couldn't see what she was really doing.

"You're not still looking up information on cancer, are you?" he asked.

Jessie didn't answer.

"Sweetheart," he said, "when your mother died it was terrible for both of us, but you don't have cancer. You're not dying!"

Jessie stared stubbornly at the floor. Truth was, cancer was the last thing on her mind right then. She had other fish to catch—if she could just find the right bait.

With a hug, her father gave up. "Get some sleep, Jess."

The next morning, Sis hummed to herself as she unlocked the cafe door. Apologizing to Vinegar hadn't been easy for her. But it sure was worth doing. She could still feel that big hug he gave her—just like he used to when he was little.

She smiled and waved at Ada Dobbins out on Main Street. Why on earth was Ada just standing there? Unless . . .

RING!

Oh, my! thought Ada, with a cautious glance at Tess—who was very busy studying the 'wildlife' on the leaves of a nearby tree.

RING! RING!

Ada took a big breath, and stepped into the phone booth. "Hello?"

A little shiver ran up her back as she listened. "Hello, Ada. I know you've bought a ticket to Atlanta. You say you want to move there and find a place to sing, *but you don't really want to move.*"

"How did you know that?" Ada demanded.

But that whispery, thundery voice wasn't answering questions. "There is someone here you've always loved. Someone you've hoped would love you back."

Ada's blue eyes were huge. *That's my secret!*

"Don't leave for Atlanta, Ada," the voice instructed. "Tell him what you feel in your heart. I'll call back when you do."

Ada's hand was shaking so hard she could barely hang up. In a daze, she started back down Main Street. In fact, if Tess hadn't been very fast on her feet, Ada would have walked right into her!

"You okay?" Tess asked.

"Oh!" said Ada, startled. "Oh, sorry. Yes . . . I'm all right." She shook her head. "Someone seems to have read my mind. Maybe . . . maybe I'm not ready to move after all."

Tess frowned. "That voice gave you some advice?"

Ada nodded absently, then walked on, leaving a puzzled Tess behind in the empty street.

An afternoon shower pattered softly against the trellis of the gazebo. Monica laughed as a playful breeze spattered her face with raindrops, which she promptly tasted.

"Imagine, Moses . . ." she told the small caterpillar sharing her book, "Georgia rain tastes just like ripe peaches!"

She flicked a stray drop from his fuzzy back. "But I'll bet it feels just plain wet to those folks." She looked across the square at the line of folding chairs outside the phone booth. There, huddled under dripping umbrellas, sat Ada, Sis, and Pearhead.

What on earth? wondered Erskine, splashing down the street. *They look just like birds on a branch—wet birds.*

Erskine stopped and placed his hands on his hips to study his soggy friends. "Aren't all of you getting carried away?"

They shrugged.

"Who do you think's making these calls?" challenged Pearhead. "Nobody could know all that stuff. Nobody but—"

31

RING!
Everyone jumped.
RING! RING!
Erskine stepped into the booth. "All right, let's see what this is all about." Grinning, he picked up the phone. "Hello, this is Erskine Hughes. And, no, we haven't got Prince Albert in a can."

But Erskine's smile quickly faded as the mysterious voice rumbled in his ear. "When your wife died your faith was shaken, and you left the ministry. Now your life feels empty."

Everyone stared at the look on Erskine's face. "Find love where you can, Erskine. Jessie needs a mother. And there's someone here wanting to be that. You know you've thought about it. You will always have wonderful memories of your wife, but she's in heaven now. And the truth is, she'd want you and Jessie to be happy again."

Erskine stood very still for a long time, then hung up. Were those tears in his eyes?

"What'd he say? What'd he say?" Pearhead wanted to know.

But Erskine just sadly shook his head and walked away.

Sis, Ada, and Pearhead looked at one another. Finally, Sis said what they were all thinking. "Folks, the voice on that phone must be God Himself!"

Under her own umbrella, Tess watched silently, her mind racing. *Surely God wouldn't . . . or would He? After all,* she thought, *angels aren't the only ones He talks to.* The puzzle was getting harder to solve.

Snuggled beside Tess under the big gold umbrella, Bits could hardly contain her excitement. *God? On the telephone? Wait till Jessie hears about this! Where is she anyway?*

Suddenly, Sis jumped up. "For heaven's sake! What are we doing sitting here like this? We've got to keep this a secret. If it gets out that God's on this phone, the whole county will be in line!"

Pearhead flew out of his chair, too. "She's right. We've got to keep our mouths shut about this."

"But what if it rings and nobody's here?" worried Ada.

"We'll take shifts," decided Sis. "I'll stay tonight. Can't sleep anyway."

Chapter Five

Shadow and Light

Bits wasn't sorry that Jessie missed all the excitement at the phone booth, because she got to tell her all about it that night. Jessie especially liked the part about the 'night watch' on the phone.

"Really?" she sputtered through a mouthful of popcorn. "All night?"

Bits loved having Jessie sleep over. There was always so much to talk about. Sometimes, she even got to help hatch one of Jessie's 'Dad and Ada' plots.

"Hey, Jess," she said, "remember the great Halloween scavenger hunt? And how tricky it was fixing who was going to be whose partner?"

Jessie grinned. "We had folks running all over the county on that one. They enjoyed it, too! 'Cept for Dad and Ada."

"Well, it wasn't your fault their car broke down in the middle of nowhere and they had to walk home," said Bits loyally. "And who'd have guessed it would rain so hard?"

"Oh well," said Jessie, looking on the bright side, "they did get to spend a lot of time together. And Ada's cold didn't last all that long."

"So what's next?" asked Bits.

"Oh, I've got an idea or two," said Jessie vaguely. "Still need a little more research, though." Then she jumped up. "How about a game of Scrabble? Oh, and did I mention that I've got to leave really early in the morning? Probably before you're awake."

"Why?" asked Bits.

"Oh, I'm . . . I'm expecting an important e-mail," said Jessie, unfolding the game board. "It's coming in real early," she added, putting out the Scrabble tiles. "You go first."

Bits looked at Jessie. *Yep, she's up to something.*

In the midnight quiet of the gazebo, Monica turned another page. "Oh, here it is!"

"Here what is?" asked Tess, suddenly at her side.

"What Mr. Plato says about how people

confuse what's real with what's not real," Monica explained.

"And how do they?" Tess asked.

"Well," Monica answered, "he says humans are like people huddled in a cave watching big shadows move across the walls. They see the shadows, but what they don't see are the real people in the sunlight outside their cave that cause those shadows. They think it's the shadows that are real. They never think to look outside, so they never see the real light.

"Oh, Tess" she said, eyes shining, "I think that may be our clue."

Tess looked a little confused.

"Don't you see?" continued Monica. "The voice on the phone is like the shadows on the cave wall. We can't know whether it's real or not until we leave the cave. And neither can the people in this town."

Tess nodded thoughtfully.

"You were right about the book helping, Tess. Isn't it wonderful how God uses every-thing and anything from bugs to Plato to inspire us!"

"Well, Angel Girl," said Tess, "inspiration is the one thing we need, 'cause it's getting worse. Folks are just sitting around waiting to be told what to do. And that's dangerous! God never wants us to stop thinking for ourselves. He gave us our minds and plenty of guidelines for living, and He wants us to use them. We're not going to get answers from some telephone!"

Beams from the sunrise flooded through the window onto Sis's sleeping face. "What?" she muttered, squeezing her eyes more tightly to shut out the morning light.

RING! RING!

"Noooooooo," she moaned, reaching out and fumbling for her alarm clock.

RING! RING!

"Not yetttttt . . ." Sis's hand stretched a little farther and bumped into the steering wheel!

The steering wheel? Sis's eyes snapped open. *What am I doing sleeping in this old pickup truck?* Then she remembered. She'd taken the night shift on 'phone watch'.

RING! RING! RING!

It's the phone!

Sis stumbled from the truck and ran for the phone. "Hello?"

"Sis. This is the new start you wanted," announced that unearthly voice.

"Oh, my," breathed Sis.

The voice rolled on. "At the end of Main Street is an empty brick building."

The old roadhouse? wondered Sis.

"Take this building and bring it to life again," the voice instructed. "You and the others. This county could use a nice supper club with good entertainment. You can run the kitchen; Pearhead can be handyman; and Ada can stay here and sing."

Oh, my! Sis stared at the phone. *Could we do it? Oh, what if we could? It would be like an answer to prayer!* She stepped from the phone booth. *Oh, my!* She began to laugh, then she started to run—right down the middle of Main Street.

Sis, Ada, and Pearhead stood in front of the old roadhouse. Eyes full of dreams, they gazed blissfully at its crumbling bricks, peeling paint, and cracked windows.

"Here, folks," announced Sis, "is our salvation." Ada and Pearhead nodded solemnly. Then they all started to grin.

What on earth . . . ? wondered Bits. She'd been watching the three of them all morning as they were jumping and shouting and running down Main Street. Staring at that falling-down old wreck of a building as if it were some kind of heavenly vision. Then off again, laughing and carrying on like crazy folks. Disturbing the doodlebugs!

Bits shook her head. *Grownups!* she thought, wandering off to find some doodlebug holes in a quieter location.

Bits had been searching for doodlebugs for more than an hour when Jessie showed up. "Caught any yet?" she asked, dropping to her knees beside Bits.

Bits shook her head. "I think they're all in hiding. Too much commotion," she grumbled, using her pine needle to point down the street at the roadhouse.

Jessie grinned. "Those folks do look a little excited," she agreed. "Why was Pearhead at the realtor's today?"

"I don't know. Something about an important letter," Bits said. "Hey, are you going to help?"

"Sure," Jessie said as she picked up a pine needle of her own. "I'll look over here."

Bits nodded happily. *Maybe with Jessie helping I'll actually catch one, before it's time for those old doodlebugs to . . .* "What is 'transformation,' Jessie?" she asked out of the blue.

"Transformation?" Jessie thought it over. "Well, remember Ada's face when she got that enormous bouquet of flowers from a 'secret admirer'?"

"Oh . . ." said Bits. "You mean the way she lit up like a sunrise?" Then she started to grin. "Or . . . do you mean that itchy rash and all the sneezing?"

"Well, really, Bits!" huffed Jessie. "How was I supposed to know she was allergic to roses?"

"More research?" teased Bits.

Jessie's lips twitched. "They were big sneezes, weren't they? And she sure gave Dad some funny looks for a while. Maybe using his initialed stationery for the note wasn't such a good idea."

Bits had to agree. That one hadn't worked out too well. "Do you think your dad and Ada will ever get together, Jess?"

"Yes!" said Jessie. "They have to. They just have to!"

Erskine was glad to see Ada so happy and full of hope. But when he found out that Sis, Ada, and Pearhead were spending all their savings on that old building . . . well, he turned out to be a real wet blanket!

"But, don't you see, Erskine," Ada tried to explain, "this is our big chance. And . . . well . . . the hand of God's in all this."

Erskine was shaking his head. "The hand of God? I don't know, Ada. I don't think that's God on the phone."

"He spoke to you, didn't He?" she pointed out.

"Someone did," Erskine answered.

Ada's eyes flashed blue fire. "Well, maybe the folks in this town believe in a more down-to-earth God than you do!"

"Yes," he said quietly, "I guess they do."

Ada was sorry she'd snapped at him. He was such a dear, good man and he sounded so defeated. She put a gentle hand on his arm. "You know, Erskine, we really miss hearing those wonderful sermons you used to give in church. Maybe we listen to a voice on the phone because we don't have you to listen to anymore."

Erskine didn't like that at all! "Seems like people would rather listen to an easy lie than a hard truth."

"Well, if that's what you think," Ada flared, "you're a coward for quitting. You should hang in there and fight, instead of losing your faith."

"I never lost my faith in God," he answered, stung by her words.

"But you lost faith in us. And that's not fair. We needed you!" Ada's voice was shaking. "Well, you just watch!"

The sleepy little town's residents woke with a start and stared in amazement. What was happening down at the old roadhouse?

Sis and Ada scrubbed and polished and planned.

Vinegar sawed and hammered and 'fixed'. (As if he'd gotten his hands on the world's biggest birdhouse, Grandpa Willis said.)

Pearhead flitted from job to job, absolutely sure that duct tape could fix anything. (Though he really did mean to go back and do a better job on that electrical wiring.)

And everybody painted.

Bits hardly knew what to watch first, and Jessie smiled a lot. There was nothing she liked better than seeing folks stop dreaming and start doing. All it took was a little gumption!

Jessie was right. Sort of. A little gumption, a lot of hard work, and three very busy weeks . . . and the job was done.

Tired, dirty, and filled to the brim with joy, the four friends stood and admired their handiwork. Windows sparkled. The oak door gleamed. And the old roadhouse wore a new coat of rosy paint. A smile passed down the line from Sis to Vinegar to Pearhead to Ada.

"We did it!" Vinegar said.

RING!

Everyone forgot to breathe.

RING! RING!

Pearhead was off down the street like a flash. He yanked the receiver from the hook. "Hello," he panted. "Hello?" he tried again. Then he held out the phone receiver—and stared at its dangling cord. "Oh, no! NO!" He'd yanked too hard! The cord was broken!

Chapter

Six

Revelations

Tess had one eye on the crowd at the phone booth—where Andrew had just arrived to fix the phone—and one eye on the dragonfly hovering right in front of her face.

"Now look," she warned, "just because I admired those rainbow wings doesn't mean I want to be your new best friend! Quit while you're ahead."

With a flick of its wings, the little flyer darted away.

"Show-off," grumbled Tess. Bits snorted, then turned it into a cough as Tess looked her way.

Across the street, Andrew squirmed in the narrow booth. Of all his assignments as an angel, this was the first time he'd been expected to fix a telephone! And it sure was hard to work with all those worried faces watching his every move. *What's so important about this phone, anyway?* he wondered.

He replaced the front panel and reached for his uniform jacket. "It's dead, all right," he said cheerfully. "I'll have to replace it."

"No!" yelled a frantic Pearhead.

"Don't do that!" Sis begged. "Can't you just rewire it?"

"I could, but a new phone will work much better," said Andrew. "You'll get a clearer connection."

"We like our connection," Ada assured him.

"Couldn't you just kinda tape it back up?" asked Pearhead.

Andrew shrugged. "Sure, if that's what you want."

They all nodded.

"And when it's fixed, stay and come to our grand opening tonight," invited Sis.

"Love to," said Andrew, rummaging in his toolbox.

"Will it take long?" fussed Pearhead. "See, this call was coming in for me, and I've gotta hear what He had to say!"

"Who?" asked Andrew.

"God," blurted Pearhead.

Andrew's eyebrows shot up. "Really?"

"Pearhead!" warned Sis with an elbow to his ribs.

"Ouch!" said Pearhead, looking at Sis. Then he turned to Andrew. "I mean, this . . . guy. It's real important!"

Bits smiled to herself as she listened. "I know what God was going to say," she whispered into her doodlebug hole.

"Oh?" said Tess, in her best tell-me-more voice.

Whoops! "Oh . . . nothing . . ." Bits mumbled, wandering off.

Hmm, thought Tess as she began to follow Bits from a distance.

Patience is a virtue! Tess reminded herself in her hiding place behind the big old oak tree. And she'd had plenty of opportunity to practice it this afternoon. Following Bits without being seen had turned into a rambling 'stop-here / look-there / oh-what's-this' trek around the whole town! Finally, the little redhead seemed to have reached her goal. With a last cautious look over her shoulder, Bits dashed up the steps and into the big white house on the corner.

Stepping from behind the old oak, Tess quietly followed her inside.

Pearhead paced back and forth outside the silent phone booth. It was fixed, the phone man had said. But he'd believe that when he heard it—

RING!

"It still works!" he shouted, zooming into the booth. "Hello . . . Hello," he panted.

"Pearhead . . ."

Tess moved quietly down the upstairs hallway to stand behind Bits.

"Pearhead . . ." said a whispery, thundery voice that sent a tingle up Tess's spine. She leaned past Bits to look inside the bedroom.

"You've done well, Pearhead," the voice rumbled on. "Enjoy your opening night."

Tess heard a click, then a dial tone. And there, looking through the big brass telescope and holding some kind of gadget up to a speakerphone, stood . . .

"Jessie!" It was pretty hard to surprise Tess, but this sure did.

With a gasp, the figure at the window spun around.

"Jessie?" repeated Tess. "You're the voice on that phone?"

"No . . . No," came the booming reply. Tess and Bits jumped—Jessie even scared herself. She looked at the voice-changer she was holding to her lips, then whipped it out of sight, but it was much too late for that now.

It was a long standoff. Tess would tap an impatient foot. Jessie would lift a stubborn chin. Neither said a word. Bits's eyes shifted back and forth between them. Then she shook her head. Interesting as it was, this silent stare-down was making her dizzy!

Finally, Tess ended it. "Now," she said sternly, "I am going to ask you once more, Jessie, and this time I expect your lips to move! Just what do you think you're doing and just who do you think you are?"

Jessie gulped. Her answer seemed to be stuck in her throat.

"She thinks she's God," Bits said helpfully.

"I do not!" protested a shocked Jessie.

"Bits, did you have anything to do with this?"

"No."

"Then you need to leave us alone and go home now, baby," said Tess.

"Okay," said Bits very quietly, and she left the room.

Tess got down to business. "Now, I have a couple of options here. I can pick you up by your ears, haul you down to the club, and force you to tell them what you've done. Or . . ."

Jessie's big eyes got even bigger.

"Or . . ." repeated Tess, folding her arms, "I can stand here and wait for you to explain yourself."

Jessie gulped. She really, truly didn't know what to say.

"I knew it wasn't God on that phone all the time," said Tess. "Now, I'll admit, I didn't know who it was, but I knew it wasn't God. You want to know how I knew?"

Jessie gave a tiny nod.

"Because God doesn't go around messing with people's lives. He gives them choices. He shows them what's right and wrong, but He lets people make up their own minds. Make their own choices."

"But what if they make the wrong ones?" Jessie asked miserably.

Ah-ha! thought Tess. "Well then, they've got to live with their bad decisions. But God is always there to help them through it. Who do you think was making a bad decision, Jessie?"

Jessie shook her head.

"Whose mind were you trying to change?" Tess pursued.

But Jessie's lips were sealed.

Backstage at the new supper club, Ada smoothed the folds of her dress with a shaking hand. It sounded like the whole county had turned out for opening night.

Why am I so nervous? she thought. *I've sung for these folks hundreds of times in church.* Then, with a laugh, Ada shook off her stage fright and stepped out into the spotlight.

"Welcome," she said, "to our grand opening."

The applause was deafening. *What was I worried about? I'm among friends.*

Ada beamed back at the crowd. "I guess you all know me, but for those who don't," she said and smiled over at Andrew, "I'm Ada Dobbins. And I want to thank you all for being here. We put our hearts and souls into this place—"

"And everything else, too!" called out Pearhead. That won more laughter and applause.

Ada laughed back. "Well, yes, I guess it does look like we took a chance. But we all had faith that it would work out." Her blue eyes went right to Erskine. "And we had faith that you all wouldn't let us down either!"

She nodded to her piano player, and a hush fell over the room as Ada's voice wove its way into the hearts of the listeners. Every eye was on the stage, and no one at all heard the snap and sizzle as the old electrical wiring began to smolder . . .

Ada knew exactly how an eagle must feel when it caught the wind and soared. She sang song after song, but she wasn't the least bit tired. The love and appreciation coming back from the audience just lifted her higher, and higher.

Together, they were creating something wonderful. So wonderful that no one noticed the smoke slipping out through the cracks in the wall!

Erskine Hughes smiled. He'd missed hearing Ada's angel voice, and he was glad that she was happy. He hadn't thought much of restoring the old roadhouse, but he had to admit it felt good to know Ada wasn't leaving. But before he could follow that thought, Ada stopped singing. And began to scream! Erskine watched in horror as flames ran up the wall behind her and smoke filled the room.

"FIRE . . . Get out!" screamed the panicked crowd. Erskine started toward the stage, but was swept back by the crowd rushing out the door.

In Jessie's room, the battle of wills was still in full swing.

"You've got to tell those people the truth, Jessie," Tess insisted.

Jessie hung her head. "I can't."

"Yes, you can," said Tess. "You just don't want to. And considering how mad they're all going to be, I can understand that."

Jessie shuddered. *Mad? They're going to kill me!*

"The fact is," said Tess, "a whole bunch of people turned their lives upside down because they thought God called them on the phone and told 'em to. They made their decisions based on a lie. And when you build a dream on sand instead of solid rock, things are going to start slipping sooner or later. Usually sooner."

"I didn't hurt anyone . . ." Jessie started, but whatever she was going to say next was lost in the scream of sirens down Main Street.

Then Bits flew into the room. "There's a fire . . . the supper club is on fire!"

Out in the street, Sis and Pearhead watched, stunned, as their dreams went up in smoke.

Erskine shoved through the crowd, his eyes searching . . . searching . . . "Did everyone get out? Where's Ada? Did anyone see Ada?" he called.

Sis looked around. "Vinegar? Vinegar!" she screamed.

Erskine started toward the burning building, then gave a joyful shout. "There they are!"

Everyone cheered as Vinegar stumbled through the door carrying Ada.

Erskine helped Vinegar place her gently on the ground. She wasn't breathing. As sirens screamed down Main Street, he bent over her small body and felt for her pulse.

Suddenly, she began to cough.

"Ada, are you okay?" Erskine asked. "Ada?"

Her only answer was another cough. And another. And then she began to breathe.

No one noticed as Andrew brushed the soot off his shirt and quietly headed for his truck, knowing she'd be okay.

Chapter Seven

Trials and Troubles

It was very quiet in Sis and Vinegar's old restaurant the next morning. Nobody there could think about anything except the fire.

Sis looked up as the screen door creaked open. "Erskine! How's Ada? Is she going to be all right?"

Erskine smiled. "Yes, thank God. But the nurse said she should stay in the hospital a couple of days. And you're a hero, you know, Vinegar. You saved Ada's life."

Vinegar stared at Erskine, amazed. He'd never been a hero before. "Anybody'd have done the same," he said shyly. "Anyway, I'm gonna be a homeless hero now. That fire burned through all our money."

Sis sighed. "I can't figure out why this happened, Erskine. What was God thinking?"

Erskine shook his head. "I'm afraid God was probably wishing that you'd all done some thinking for yourselves, instead of taking orders from some stranger over the phone."

"I'm only gonna say this once, Erskine," Sis answered. "You gave up your chance to preach. Maybe God started calling us up because there wasn't anybody else around to tell us the truth anymore!"

Erskine looked down in shame. He knew she was right. He had let his congregation down. "God didn't do this, Sis," he said quietly.

The screen door creaked again. "Hi, everybody," said a raspy little voice.

Erskine jumped up. "Ada!"

Ada smiled at her startled friends. "I was just running up a hospital bill I couldn't pay, so I left."

"You sure you're okay?" Erskine asked.

"Right as rain," she answered, "just a little hoarse." She hesitated a moment. "I came by to say that . . . I think I'm going to try Atlanta after all."

Nobody knew what to say—especially Erskine.

Tess dropped a quarter into the pay phone and dialed.

Alone in her room Jessie tried to ignore the ringing phone. But whoever it was wasn't giving up. She cautiously lifted the receiver. "Hello?"

"How are you doing, baby?" asked Tess.

Jessie could barely speak. "Ada? Is she . . . ?"

"She's going to be fine," said Tess quickly. "She's up and around and still has a chance at that job in Atlanta."

"Can't they fix the supper club?" Jessie asked hopefully.

"No," said Tess. "It's gone."

Tears filled Jessie's eyes. *It's all my fault!*

"Jessie?" said Tess. "I know you're scared. But you can't keep holding this secret in or it'll eat you up inside." Tess waited, but there was no answer. "It's going to be hard to tell these folks the truth, but remember our deal. I'll be right there with you. Now, you get down here to Sis and Vinegar's. I'm waiting."

Jessie sat very still, her mind racing. Then she straightened her shoulders and answered, "Okay."

Tess hung up, stepped from the phone booth, and nearly tripped over Pearhead! He was back in his chair, right outside the door.

Tess frowned. "Shouldn't you be getting some rest?"

Pearhead shook his head. "I'm waiting for God to call and explain all this."

Tess's eyes flashed. "God did not call on this phone. He never did, Pearhead. That's not how He works!"

"Don't say that," Pearhead begged. "Don't take it away from me! I know I'm not very smart. Everybody makes fun of me." His words tumbled out almost faster than Tess could listen. "Then one day God picked me—me!—to call up on the phone and talk to! It made me feel . . . well, like there was a reason I'd been born." He looked at Tess with sad eyes. "Nobody's born just so people can make fun of them, are they?"

"No, Pearhead," Tess said tenderly, "nobody's born to be made fun of. You are one of God's beautiful creations, and He loves you. Exactly as you are."

But Pearhead just shook his head and walked away.

Chapter Eight

Moment of Truth

It wasn't at all quiet inside Sis and Vinegar's old restaurant that afternoon, which was too bad because now all the voices were angry ones.

Sis glared at Pearhead. "You're the one who started all this!"

"Me!" Pearhead glared right back. "You're the one who said to rebuild that place."

"God said to," Sis snapped.

Erskine slammed his hand on the table. "That's ridiculous! Ada could have died because of this stupidity."

"If anybody was stupid, it was me for listening to Sis!" shouted Pearhead.

Sis looked ready to explode. "How dare you! We lost everything we own in that fire. Our whole future. We're stuck here now!"

That set Pearhead off again. "What about me? I lost my truck. My nest egg's gone. I'm as good as buried!"

All at once, the room was very quiet. They looked at one another, ashamed of the things they'd said.

The screen door squeaked as Tess entered. Pearhead sank into a chair. "Maybe God'll call . . ." he offered in a dejected voice.

"Well," said Ada, "all I know is, I've hit the end of the line here."

Erskine's voice was very tired. "Looks like we all have."

Bits peeked through the screen door. But, for once, she wasn't sure she wanted to know what was going on. She slipped across the room and handed Ada an envelope.

"This is from Jessie," she whispered. Then she zipped back out the door—before any of that old gloom could stick to her.

Ada opened the letter and began to read aloud: "Dear Ada. It's me, Jessie. I guess we're both leaving town . . ."

Her listeners traded alarmed looks.

"Dear Lord in heaven," breathed Tess.

Ada continued reading: "I wanted to tell you and everybody that it wasn't God on the telephone. It was me."

"What?" they all shouted.

As shocked as everyone else, Ada read on:

"I was the voice on the phone. I never meant to hurt anybody, but it looks like I ruined everybody's life. Now, I think I really must be dying, 'cause I've never hurt so much inside in my whole life."

Ada's eyes filled with tears. "Anyway, I did have a good reason. I did it because—"

Ada stopped as she saw the next words. *Oh, Jessie!* Her eyes raced down the page. *Oh, dear. This is nobody's business but mine!*

She cleared her throat and skipped down to the end of the letter: "Because . . ." she made up, ". . . well, I had a good reason. At least I thought so. Anyway, maybe I'll see you on the road. Give my dad a kiss good-bye. Jessie."

There was a stunned silence, then everyone talked at once.

"That voice on the phone was Jessie?" Erskine repeated.

"What was she thinking?" asked Sis.

"She said she had a good reason," reminded Vinegar.

"I'm sure she thought she did," Ada said quietly.

"Nothing excuses this," said Erskine, half angry, half worried. "I'm so sorry about everything that happened." He stood up. "I've got to find her! I don't know what else to do."

Tess stepped in. "Yes, you do, Erskine. Everybody here says you used to be a man of God. Well, you still are, if you want to be. You already know the best way to bring that little girl home," Tess said urgently. "Every worthwhile search begins with God. Because whatever you're looking for, and wherever it is, God is already there."

Tess's words touched Erskine's weary spirit like a comforting hand. He bowed his head, and turned back to God, who had never turned away from him.

"Lord," he prayed, "please take care of my girl. Send an angel right now to find her and bring her home. Amen," he finished humbly.

For just a moment the little cafe felt like a church. Everyone smiled. Their pastor was back.

Then Pearhead—the old Pearhead—jumped up. "Well, you're a little rusty, but it's good to hear you praying again, Preacher." He bounced around the room, excitedly barking out orders. "We've got to find Jessie. Okay, everybody, let's go. We'll look everywhere!"

To everyone's amazement, Vinegar stepped forward and took charge. "Pearhead, let's organize this search. Sis, you go west . . ."

Tess stood in the empty restaurant, her face sad. She had her own words to say to her Lord: "I know You'll send an angel to that girl, Father. One who won't let You down this time."

Monica looked up as a shadow fell across the page she was reading.

"Tess? What happened?" she asked.

Tess sighed. "I blew it is what happened, Angel Girl."

"You? Blew it?" Monica repeated.

"Yes. Me," she said. "I tried to lead a little girl to the light of truth, and I pushed when I should've pulled, and pulled when I should've pushed. Now everybody knows some of the truth and nobody knows all of it."

Monica could tell that Tess was very upset with herself. How could she help? She looked down at her book. Suddenly, she knew!

"Tess!" she said, her eyes shining, "I think God just turned on a light for us!"

And, indeed, it seemed He had—a brilliant light that filled the gazebo, painting the walls with perfect shadows of Tess and Monica!

"Remember, Tess, what Mr. Plato said about how people are so busy looking at shadows on a wall that they never see the real light at all? That's what's happening here!

"You sent a little girl outside to face the light, Tess. But that isn't enough. I've been watching these people. You need to let light in on the whole town. And Jessie is your starting point."

But Tess saw one very big problem with this wonderful solution. "Jessie has run away."

"Ah," said Monica, "has she? Where do people go, Tess, when they can't stand too much light?"

Tess thought for a moment, then she began to smile, too. "To the dark."

Monica nodded. "And there's one place I can think of around here that's definitely been missing the light," she said as she looked across the town square to the abandoned church.

Tess gave Monica a huge hug. And she even smiled at the little caterpillar. "Angel Girl," she said, "you've done your job very well—brilliantly, in fact!"

Chapter Nine

Seeing the Light

The forlorn little figure in the front pew jumped as the church doors 'whooshed' open. Then Jessie shrugged, and went back to staring at . . . nothing.

Tess slipped into the pew beside her. "You used to come here a lot, didn't you?" she said softly.

Jessie nodded.

"Then your whole life got turned upside down," Tess went on.

"Leave me alone," ordered Jessie.

Tess shook her head. "I can't do that, baby."

Tears filled Jessie's eyes. "Why not? I'm used to it."

"You feel you're alone," Tess said gently, "but that's not reality, Jessie. That's just a shadow on the wall. God always has a plan, but He doesn't always hand it to us on a silver platter. Sometimes, we have to learn that the hard way, baby. We all have to."

"But how can you be sure that's true?" asked Jessie, who always had to understand exactly how things worked.

Tess smiled. "Because I'm an angel."

Jessie stared at the radiant light surrounding the . . . the bug lady! "How are you doing that?" Jessie asked. "Unless . . . you really are an—"

Tess nodded. "An angel, Jessie, sent by God to tell you that He loves you, sweetheart. Through all your loss and every mistake, God loves you."

That was just too much for Jessie. Her tears overflowed. "He must be the only one."

Tess hugged her. "No," she said firmly. "A whole lot of people love you. Take a look." She turned Jessie toward the back of the church. There stood Bits and Sis and Pearhead and Vinegar . . . and her father.

"But how?" Jessie turned back to Tess. But her angel was gone and she was in her daddy's arms.

"She's okay!" shouted Pearhead.

"What a relief," said Sis. Then her tone changed. "But that was a terrible thing to do, 'Miss Fix-it'!"

"You've ruined us," added Vinegar.

"Somebody ought to tan your hide," growled Pearhead, ready to volunteer.

"How did you do it?" asked Sis. "That deep voice?"

Seeing the Light

Jessie could practically smell the tar and feathers! "You . . . you can buy a toy microphone that changes your voice."

"And where'd you dig up all that personal information?" Pearhead wanted to know.

"My computer," Jessie confessed, with a nervous look at her father. "Hacking. E-mail. Then, I saw Sis's letter from the bank, and Bits hears things. And with my telescope I can see the phone from my window. It wasn't that hard."

"But why?" asked her father. "Why did you do this, Jessie?"

Jessie hung her head. "Because . . . because Ada loves you, Dad."

"WHAT?" Erskine's shocked question was written all over the other faces, too. Except for Sis, whose lips twitched, and Bits, who just looked very interested in what would happen next.

"She does!" insisted Jessie. "Nobody makes Ada smile like you do. But you didn't see it, and she couldn't even see you on Sundays in church anymore. So she gave up. She was moving away!

"So," she explained, "I figured if Ada had a

real good reason to stay here, maybe she wouldn't move. 'Cause whether you want to believe it or not, I'm dying! After I'm gone I don't want you to be alone."

Erskine pulled his daughter close. "Oh, Jessie, you're not dying. You're not!"

But Jessie's mind was made up. "Yes, I am, just like Mom."

"No," he insisted. "No. No. NO!"

"Yes, I am."

They might have gone on like that the rest of the day—if not for the glowing light that filled the little church with glory. And at the heart of the radiance stood Tess.

"Oh my Lord . . ." breathed Jessie's father.

Tess smiled. "I'm an angel, Erskine. Sent by God."

"God has returned to this church," he said with awe.

"He never left," corrected Tess. "But some of you have been missing. Look at what went on here. You thought you heard God on a pay phone. And you all wanted something out of it for yourselves."

Everyone looked a little uncomfortable.

"I can't say what Jessie did was right," Tess went on. "But at least she was trying to make things better for other folks. You've all been hunkering down in your holes like doodlebugs expecting God to reach in and pull you out, instead of reaching to Him with a little faith."

"We had faith," protested Sis. "We believed. We followed."

"Followed who?" asked Tess. "God doesn't want blind faith. He wants you to know exactly who you're putting your trust in."

"So that's it, then," said a deflated Pearhead. "We let somebody else do our thinking for us and now everything's a mess."

Tess studied their dejected faces. Then she smiled, and showed them what they hadn't seen for themselves.

"Well, now," she said, "God has a way of working things out for those who love Him. Sis, you did something big, girl. Don't forget that."

Yes! thought Sis. *I did! We all did. With just grit and gumption!*

"Vinegar . . ." Tess had a special smile for

him. "You became a hero and earned the respect you've always wanted." She turned. "And, Pearhead, you did something very smart."

"I did?" he asked, surprised.

Tess nodded. "Remember those papers you sent in?"

"Oh . . ." he said, a light dawning. "Oh, my! The insurance!"

"Insurance?!" squealed Sis. "You bought insurance on our building, Pearhead?"

"Well, the realtor suggested it, and it seemed like a good idea," he explained. "But with all that was going on I clean forgot I'd done it."

There was an awed silence.

"And, Erskine," Tess said gently, "a good woman loves you and an empty church misses you."

Tess let her words sink in before turning to the girl who had started it all.

"And you, Jessie. Believe me when I tell you this: *You are not dying.* Lots of children lose their mamas and get ideas like that. But you are going to have a long, wonderful life with your daddy . . . and whoever else."

Jessie knew she was hearing the truth. With her eyes and heart full of hope and belief, she looked at Tess. But Jessie knew her dad still needed Ada. After all, when she joined the astronaut program her dad would still be alone. Unless . . .

Tess—who knew exactly what and who Jessie was thinking about—winked. "No time for schemes right now, Jessie. There's still a little unfinished business. You owe these good people a real apology, because they deserve the chance to forgive you."

Jessie nodded. Fair was fair. "Pearhead, I'm sorry. And Sis and Vinegar, I'm sorry for all the trouble I caused. I'll make it up to you all. Somehow. Someday." In fact, she already had an idea . . .

"You just did, sugar," Sis said quickly. She could tell that busy brain was already hard at work. "We'll get by." And they would!

Last of all, Jessie turned to her father. "I'm sorry, Dad."

He just hugged her, and said the best words of all. "I love you, Jessie."

Chapter Ten

Transformations

*R*ING! RING! RING!

The old pay phone vibrated impatiently. But the folks on the church steps had other things to think about.

"You know," said Pearhead, "it wouldn't take all that much to get our church back to the way it used to be . . ."

RING! RING! RING!

The pay phone echoed inside Sis and Vinegar's, too. But Ada was too busy rereading Jessie's letter to notice.

"Ada?"

Her hands tightened on the page. Then she looked up with a smile for Erskine, and saw Jessie, too.

"Oh, sweetheart," she said, hugging Jessie tight, "you're all right! I read them your letter." Ada glanced at Erskine. "Only part of it, though."

Erskine smiled. "I know about the other

part. I guess I've known about the other part for a long time. I . . . I hope you'll stay, Ada."

Ada didn't answer right away. It's hard to talk when you can't breathe. "Yes, I'd like that," she finally got out.

Triumphant, Jessie gave them both a hug and ran off to find Bits.

"Bits, do you know what's even better than catching doodlebugs?"

Bits looked up at Tess, "No what?"

"Seeing what happens when it's time for doodlebugs to find the light," said Tess. "Watch . . ."

"Can I watch, too?" asked Jessie, kneeling beside them.

Then . . . "OH!" breathed Bits, as a tiny cloud of rainbow-winged flyers burst from the darkness—to dance in the light.

Her eyes full of wonder, Bits looked up at Tess. "Transformation?" she asked softly.

Tess's answering smile was like a prayer.

"Yes, baby. That's what happens when some-thing becomes what God meant it to be all along."

The two girls and Tess watched with de-light as the cloud of shimmering wings spi-raled upward. Swirling and spinning like joy made visible—following a snow-white dove into the light.